Gangs of The Big Smoke

Michele Albanese

Published by New Generation Publishing in 2022

Copyright © Michele Albanese 2022

First Edition

The author asserts the moral right under the Copyright, Designs and Patents Act 1988 to be identified as the author of this work.

All Rights reserved. No part of this publication may be reproduced, stored in a retrieval system or transmitted, in any form or by any means without the prior consent of the author, nor be otherwise circulated in any form of binding or cover other than that which it is published and without a similar condition being imposed on the subsequent purchaser.

ISBN
      Paperback   978-1-80369-301-9
      Ebook   978-1-80369-302-6

www.newgeneration-publishing.com

New Generation Publishing

Chapter One

The Beginnings

Organised crime in London in the early 1900s was complicated. There were twenty-five different corrupt raffles, numerous bookmakers, lots of prostitutes and pimps, protection rackets (extortion), ice cream wars, professional shoplifters, robbery, counterfeiting, debt collection and pickpocketing. Borders changed and gangs would often change their leaders.

There was no need to go into opium, cocaine and cannabis distribution, as it was too widely available in pharmacies. It was also quite expensive to buy. Most of it was consumed by the rich, powerful and famous. Occasionally it trickled down to the prostitutes, the pimps and the poor.

There were lots of Jews, Germans, Italians and Irish - it really was a melting pot of disorganised crime. The Jews couldn't work on a Saturday. The Germans and the Irish drank too much on a Friday and the Italians were more interested in their pasta sauce - it needed an Englishman.

In 1901, Mr Smith owned seventy-three houses in Soho (but he never called it 'Soho' he called it 'South of Houston Street') and twenty-one houses in Holborn. He would get a horse and carriage to The Dorchester hotel to have his lunch every day;

he hated dining alone. The Dorchester had Italian staff, as did most of the top hotels and he would engage with them. He grew up with the Italians in Clerkenwell, Islington since the 1860s. The Italians when meeting each other would use the surname a lot.

Mr Smith could have brought his security men with him but he decided not to because he didn't like them. They would be better off collecting a shilling a week for his rent which is what he charged for his properties. He wanted to sack them. He didn't want protection gangs in Soho.

When he dined alone he would buy *The Times* to keep him company. (He bought *The Times* a lot).

Deep down he wanted to be looked after by an Italian family who would cook and clean for him.

Charley Sabini worked in The Dorchester every day. He was a waiter. He was a lot younger than Mr Smith and they would later get on really well. In fact Mr Smith would insist on Charley Sabini serving him every day. That day he had seafood linguine.

Charley Sabini had grandiose ambitions for himself. He didn't know anything about organised crime. He was only twenty-five compared to Mr Smith who was in his sixties.

"Do you want a house in Soho?," Mr Smith asked Charley Sabini.

He was flabbergasted at by this proposal. "I will tell you after you finish your apple pie and ice cream," Charley said to Mr Smith.

"I finish at two o'clock," said Charley Sabini to Mr Smith.

"OK, we will meet at the bar after," said Mr Smith.

Caruso was a pimp who would fall in love with his prostitutes - that's why he was not a very good pimp but he was learning. He wanted to go into other things. He was friends with Charley Sabini. One prostitute told him to go into bookmaking and casino corruption but Caruso couldn't because you needed money and a gang for that sort of thing. Both Sabini and him lived in Clerkenwell. He was good friends with Sabini. Sabini thought Caruso would make an adequate pimp if he didn't fall in love with them.

The meeting began with Mr Smith saying to Charley Sabini:

"I think there is a lot of disorganised crime and London is crying out for a gang to dominate for the next.30 years. What I need you to do is to find me a family I can spend the rest of my life with. What

I can do is set you up with good money and what you must do is bring about twenty members of your gang to Brighton racecourse where you will collect fifty per cent of the profit from the bookmakers and ten per cent goes to me."

"I'm... speechless," said Sabini.

"What about your family?," asked Mr Smith.

Mr Smith wanted to live with a family and eat with others. He had made his money buying cheap property in Soho when it was rife with bubonic plague. He was also lucky with the only racehorse he ever owned. He sold it to a stud for hundreds of pounds. The horse was unbeaten and still earned him money for stud fees. It was called 'South of Houston Street.'

Sabini said to Mr Smith, "I will arrange a family for you. I don't earn enough money here and plus I've never been to Brighton."

Mr Smith offered to give Sabini a hundred pounds and Sabini left to go home and think about his recruitment drive and learn.

Mr Smith wasn't stupid and knew he would make a lot of money with his alliance with Sabini.

The first person Sabini spoke to was Caruso.

"Caruso I've got the money to start up a gang."

"What sort of gang?," asked Caruso.

"A money-making gang," said Sabini and then he went on and said, "We are going to start off with pimping, raffle tickets and bookmakers in Brighton and then we will get into the numbers racket in London and prostitution now."

Caruso was definitely interested and wanted to know how many people Sabini needed.

"I need twenty people and a couple of policemen" was the response.

Sabini didn't know much about protection rackets.

Although Sabini had spent most of his working life in The Dorchester, Mr Smith had taught him about the raffle, permission for prostitution and horseracing. He thought it was a good idea to first take Brighton's bookmakers, then Kempton Park, then Sandown and finally the whole of the south.

He wondered if it was a good idea to host Mr Smith with his family or go to another family. Time stood still in the moment. He had to get the gang and policemen on his side. Two of the possible members had to know policemen where the policemen could get paid to turn a blind eye.

Caruso was recruiting and Sabini was looking forward to tomorrow's shift at The Dorchester where he could talk to Mr Smith about the policemen, Brighton and the three-storey house in Soho which would act as headquarters for his collective. Also, he would talk about protection rackets away from Soho and raffle tickets. He knew he had to have a showdown eventually with the Germans in Farringdon.

Chapter Two

Headquarters

Mr Smith was late on this day. Again he came on his own. He was happy to see Sabini and Sabini was even happier to see him. The two had a conversation about the rise of the motor car and the fact they were being built in France and Germany.

Sabini then asked Mr Smith if he would like to live with his family.

In which Mr Smith said, "I think it would be best if he lived with another family, so as not to mix business with pleasure."

He was a whiley old businessman. Sabini then asked what was the best way to take over Brighton's bookmakers. Mr Smith liked Sabini's questions.

"What you do is to stop them from taking bets. Then agree that you take fifty per cent of the net profit and give me ten per cent. You will need a large gang to make it work."

"I need a couple of policemen in London as well, let me get your chicken," said Sabini.

Whilst Sabini was away, Mr Smith thought about his policeman friend who would be ideal to work with. He would organise a meeting with Sabini and himself to smooth over the raffle and other revenue streams.

Sabini brought the chicken and broccoli.

"Mr Smith?," said Sabini, "I'd like to introduce prostitution into The Dorchester and The Ritz."

"That's a brilliant idea," said Mr Smith "and what I'm gonna do for you is let you meet some friends from the police force and I want ten per cent of the prostitution money."

Sabini knew that he had to leave working in The Dorchester, but before he left he had to smooth the path for the prostitutes to enter The Dorchester and then The Ritz. He finished at two o'clock and would have to speak to the manager who was Italian as well.

Sabini asked Mr Smith what house and what street his new residence would be on.

"27 Wardour Street," said Mr Smith. "It's got three floors and three bedrooms. It will house about eighteen to twenty."

The plan was coming along nicely. Sabini could not believe his luck. No more having to wake up at five. No more having to walk miles to work. No more serving diners he didn't like. But he thought about the problems he had to face. He thought loyalty was a prerequisite. Later he would meet Caruso to see how many men he could raise. But now he would have to hand in his notice to the manager and ask him if he could turn The Dorchester into a semi brothel.

He knocked on the manager's door.

"I love The Dorchester but I have to leave," said Sabini. Then he continued, "I'm only twenty-five and I want to work in ice cream."

"Why don't you stay here - I will give you a pay rise," said the manager.

"Can I give you a pay rise?," asked Sabini.

"What do you mean?," said the manager.

"I just want to bring a few girls into the bar - they are classy girls and well-behaved, some turn a few tricks but I will give you a pound a day. Who knows, you might even get off with one of them, especially if I give the word," said Sabini.

"I will need a password so they can get in," said the manager.

They agreed that the password would be 'Sabini girl' and they would start this weekend.

Charley Sabini was happy with the day's events, he would link up with Caruso tonight and would have lunch with Mr Smith tomorrow.

Chapter Three

Recruitment Drive and Raffle Tickets

So far Sabini and Caruso could only raise eleven men. Sabini would try the restaurants for waiters and cooks. He got lucky and raised two more. That made a total of thirteen. The Brighton races were only a week away. He gave each man a pound for a week's wages.

Caruso was busy getting the right girls for The Dorchester on Friday night. It was happening and the whole gang moved into the house in Soho over the next few days.

Sabini moved out of his house and let his parents know that if they needed anything he was there. His mum cried when he said he was leaving.

The men had to sleep three to a room. They knew it was only temporary. They were all ready for Brighton but for now, they would concentrate on the lucrative raffle market and prostitution. Brighton was in nine days.

Soho and Mayfair were close to each other. Mayfair didn't generate as much wealth for the raffle as Soho did. The gang found a printer in Faringdon. The printer offered good terms. Sabini could pay it back after the raffle.

Sabini held a meeting. He wanted to know what the best day for a raffle would be and how much a ticket would be. They all congregated in the communal lounge in Soho. It was a Thursday and they all agreed that next Thursday would be a good time to draw the numbers. The tickets would be a penny each. The winner would collect fifty per cent of the intake. He made Bastino head of the raffle ticket operation - that was due to the way he could talk to strangers. He put the gang in pairs to sell the raffle tickets.

Sabini looked forward to speaking to Mr Smith tomorrow at The Dorchester. Everybody had an early night and was careful not to crease their newly bought clothes. They were all starving and agreed that each one would take it in turn to make a pasta sauce, as they all had refused to go to China Town to eat.

Most of them slept well. Sabini woke up first and decided to buy three dozen eggs and thirty rashers of bacon. He had to buy a pan as well as fifteen plates and cutlery. He returned to the house and most of the other thirteen were up. The plan for the day was for him to meet Mr Smith, sell the raffle tickets and sort out the prostitutes for The Dorchester that night.

The gang devoured their breakfast. They talked about who would cook the pasta sauce that evening; finding tomatoes was more difficult than selling raffle tickets! He might have to go back to The Dorchester to get tomatoes in a jar. Anyway for now he would issue 240 raffle tickets to each gang member. That would make exactly a pound in revenue. You can times that by fifteen which would make fifteen pounds. Sabini decided on five pounds for the winner and ten pounds for the gang.

It was getting close to lunchtime at The Dorchester. Mr Smith decided to walk. He knew he had left Soho when he could see fewer people. The houses in Mayfair made him jealous. He breathed in the air. He was determined to make this gang work.

Mr Smith was already at The Dorchester when Sabini arrived.

"Just in time to order," said Mr Smith.

"I will have the same as you," said Sabini.

"Mackerel, potatoes and vegetables," said Mr Smith to the waiter.

"I'll have the same," said Sabini.

The conversation turned to the Brighton racecourse again and the next race meeting was next Monday according to *The Times*. "We will make it work," said Sabini.

"I have confidence in you," said Mr Smith.

Sabini decided to speak to the manager of The Dorcester about the sale of raffle tickets in the hotel and about tonight's prostitution. The manager sat down at the table with Mr Smith and Sabini. It was news to Mr Smith who really wanted to know what family he would be staying at. Sabini said it was being taken care of. He was really thinking of distributing to all of the hotels, restaurants and coffee bars and giving them all twenty per cent. Forty per cent would go to his organisation and forty per cent to the winner.

The manager agreed. Sabini asked the manager if he could telegram all of the other hotels to see if they would come on board too.

Meanwhile back on the streets, the gang members didn't do that well at selling raffle tickets except for Bastini who approached restaurants and coffee bars. He had the same idea as Sabini at the same time.

Chapter Four

Harlots

It was Friday night and Caruso had handpicked his six prostitutes for The Dorchester. He needed two carriages. Sabini came along. He had been in The Dorchester nearly all day, now it could be all night as well. The doorman had let them all in under the password of 'Sabini's girls'.

The bar was packed with well-heeled gentlemen who had just come back from the races at Sandown. Most worked on the stock exchange or had their own businesses. There were quite a few guests who were staying the night. Guinness was a popular drink. The girls with Sabini and Caruso drank gin and Schweppes. Sabini drank neat vodka and Caruso drank whiskey and water.

The girls looked stunning and the men in the club offered their barstools to the girls. There were other girls there with their boyfriends. One couple started arguing because her boyfriend was leering at one of the girls. Julia copped off with one of the men and they went back to his room. He paid her a pound for an hour; he was only there for forty minutes. Julia wanted to give the money to Sabini who had previously told her to "just give me the money at the end of the night".

Things had started quickly and brilliantly. The manager had to start renting rooms by the hour. All the girls were busy and business was good. Sabini and Caruso spent a lot of time on their own while the girls worked.

It was now eleven o'clock and they must have collected at least thirty-five pounds. The bar was still packed and Sabini thought about doing the same thing at The Ritz. All he had to do was ask the manager to smooth the way for him. Sabini wanted to go home to speak to the rest of the gang who he could trust with the money.

Sabini arrived home by carriage about midnight. Quite a few of the gang were still up and he knew every person who was awake and in the communal lounge would be talking about how well Bastoni had done selling raffle tickets to cafés and restaurants on a sale or on a return basis. They would concentrate on spreading their net further until they had the whole of London. Sabini would make Bastoni head of raffle tickets. They would do the draw on Wednesday so the result could go in Thursday's newspapers.

The gang asked how it went in The Dorchester that night. Sabini said it went brilliantly and that they had made thirty-five pounds in the first three hours. Caruso reckoned he might be there until five am. They were making money and were still waiting on Brighton to make even more money.

Saturday was like Friday - much the same. Raffle tickets and prostitution. Sabini thought the Germans and the Jews had to be taken out. He made his way to The Dorchester. He called Caruso and Bastoni. The horse carriage pulled up. Caruso had to get the girls for another lucrative night. Sabini walked in with Bastoni. Bastoni wanted a pint of Guinness. Sabini was on vodka. It wasn't as busy as last night. Sabini wanted to make Bastoni joint second-in-command with Caruso. He wanted to commence a chain of command.

Sabini asked Bastoni, "how do we get rid of the Germans?"

"That's a good question," said Bastoni.

"What do you think?," asked Sabini.

"I tell you what I think. Go onto their turf in Farringdon, where they do the raffle, and take over the raffle market. This will cause conflict and then incite violence. We take out the Germans and then take Farringdon. They have about twenty fighters."

At that point, the same six girls walked in with Caruso who gave Sabini ninety-five pounds in takings from the previous night. He gave the girls ten pounds each and put thirty-five pounds in for the organisation. Bastoni thought it was too much to give. So did Caruso. Sabini argued that you can buy loyalty. Julia was already being chatted up. Sabini gave the manager a pound who had telegrammed The Ritz informing them of Sabini and Bastoni's imminent arrival.

Sabini wanted to go to The Ritz with Bastoni because he wanted to install six more prostitutes. He would leave Caruso in charge of the girls. Caruso by now had refused to fall in love with the girls. He didn't want to lose face with himself. Sabini didn't even tell him that he was joint second-in-command. Sabini and Caruso left The Dorchester and walked to The Ritz. They passed Mayfair and Piccadilly. It was a warm evening and the London sky was almost scarlet.

They arrived after five minutes and the doorman said, "Mr Sabini and Mr Bastoni?"

"Yes," said the two. They felt important. They went into the bar and it was busier than The Dorchester. Again they ordered a pint of Guinness and a double vodka. Sabini hated the fact that his lieutenant drank an Irish drink but Sabini couldn't really talk as he was having a German drink.

"Shall we start drinking vino from now on?," asked Sabini to Bastoni.

"Yes, we will start tomorrow. We are Italian Caruso. My father would go mad," Sabini said.

They were both relaxed and comfortable in each other's company. Bastoni talked to Sabini about the raffle takings. They were not that good - they only accumulated two pounds and sixty-eight pence. Sabini said we will have to keep the prize money.

"Love your corruption," said Bastoni.

Business in The Dorchester was not as good as it was last night. Caruso had to stop himself from falling in love. The girls had some cocaine which they called 'white snuff'. Caruso knew all about it as all the gangsters knew about it too. You couldn't make money from it though because the pharmacies had it all sewn up. The six girls all took some and offered some to Caruso who kindly refused. Julia took some at the bar because it was legal like normal snuff. There were a few of the men who were coked off their faces. Caruso felt left out. He wasn't good at being a pimp but the girls loved him, so he must have been doing something right. It wasn't like this last night. Caruso missed Sabini and Bastoni.

The girls were working well when about fifteen men walked in.

"Yippee," said Julia. She was at the bar drinking gin and Schweppes. She couldn't care less about the business that night and quite fancied her pimp, Caruso.

The time was 11 pm. The Ritz was mellow and Sabini and Bastoni were guessing who was the drunkest at the bar. They started talking about how to deal with the Germans. They knew the Germans would drink in The Hoop and Grapes in Farringdon.

They would go on Tuesday night. There would be a maximum of fifteen Germans. Sabini had to recruit more to boost his numbers up. They would storm the pub and win the biggest melee London had seen in years.

Bastoni asked, "what if the Germans had guns?"

Sabini replied and said that he would buy muskets. It was war.

Sabini wanted to go back to The Dorchester and so did Bastoni. They walked the short journey. They would speak to The Ritz manager through The Dorchester manager about prostitutes. He needed more men for the fight. His army would be paid a pound each. He also needed the police on his side and to find a family for Mr Smith.

Chapter Five

The Ritz Comes on Board

It was Monday and Sabini had organised a family for Mr Smith to live with. He went to The Dorchester early. He had a late breakfast of kippers and eggs and bread and butter with a cup of coffee. The gang were busy selling raffle tickets to shops, cafés, hotels and pubs.

The family Sabini asked for were a good family. They were called the Santaniello family with a boy of fourteen. They rented a small house in Clerkenwell. Mr Smith owned a large house in

Islington where The Santaniellos would move into.

Sabini had finished his breakfast and was waiting for Mr Smith. The manager of The Dorchester came and sat down next to Sabini. Sabini gave him three pounds for his role in smoothing the path for the prostitutes to operate on Friday, Saturday and Sunday as was arranged.

"Thanks for letting me operate the girls this weekend, I really appreciated it. Can I ask you for another favour?," Sabini said.

The manager was quiet.

Sabini continued, "I want to operate in every high-class hotel in London. I will pay you good money. I want The Ritz next."

The manager said, "We can go to The Ritz this afternoon."

"Deal," said Sabini.

It was within walking distance. Mr Smith arrived from his half-hour carriage ride from Islington.

"Hello Charley," said Mr Smith.

"Hello Mr Smith," said Sabini.

The two were happy to see each other. Mr Smith especially. The manager came over and said, "lunch is on me."

Sabini said, "I will be the waiter."

Mr Smith loved the attention. Everything seemed too good to be true. Sabini took the order and Mr Smith ordered roast pork and cabbage and boiled potatoes slightly sautéed in English butter. Sabini ordered a twenty-eight day aged steak (medium rare) with fried potatoes and broccoli. Sabini put the order to the kitchen and went back. Once a waiter, always a waiter he thought. He gave Mr Smith a percentage of the prostitute takings (about ten per cent).

The lunch was delicious. Sabini had a glass of red wine and Mr Smith had a scotch. The manager felt a little nervous as he was paying for the lunch and did not want them to drink too much. Sabini asked the manager if he could offload two hundred raffle tickets for him. Then he asked Mr Smith about protection rackets and how he would go about it. They got another drink.

Mr Smith said, "It's all sewn up, you have to take over an enemy's turf. Soho, I think, is the only territory that has no protection rackets. Chinatown has made sure of that. The Chinese keep themselves to themselves."

Then Mr Smith went on to say that he was the biggest fish in Soho and he would advocate the reason for protection money. Sabini thought about the fight with the Germans and the spoils of war tomorrow night. Sabini asked Mr Smith about the availability of policemen.

"We will talk tomorrow," said Mr Smith.

Sabini thought about installing many girls in the best hotels in London. He waited by himself for The Dorchester manager to arrive so they could turn up at The Ritz. Sabini had another glass of red wine. He knew tomorrow night would be a big night with the confrontation with the Germans.

The manager finally came. It was only a short walk to The Ritz. Sabini felt a little merry. They walked into The Ritz and Sabini had another glass of red wine. The Dorchester manager had the same.

In came the Ritz manager who said, "Hello what do you want?"

The Dorchester manager said, "this is Charley Sabini."

The three men decided to go to a private table.

"We have a transportable brothel and we can pay you three hundred and sixty-five pounds per year. All the girls are sheer class. Sometimes they might need rooms for an hour. It's usually half an hour if they are willing to pay but it might be for the whole night," said Sabini.

The Dorchester manager said to The Ritz manager, "I'm in."

The Ritz manager said, "so am I."

And with that, the deal was done. Sabini wanted to go home and talk tactics about how to take the Germans. The Dorchester manager wanted to have a drink. Sabini stayed for another hour then went home, as he missed Caruso, Bastoni and the others.

As he walked home back to Soho, he had a good think. He had never done this before. It was all very well taking out twelve to fifteen Germans but what about after? They will come back thought Sabini. And what about the protection money? The rest of the Germans would still collect it. There were coffee houses, restaurants, ironmongers, butchers, greengrocers, haberdashers, tailors and bakers.

He arrived home and there were about eight of the group in the house. The others in the were out selling raffle tickets. Sabini thought he would hold the meeting when the rest came back. He also thought about having a girlfriend. Some of the gang had girlfriends but they never brought them back to their Soho home. He also thought about asking Mr Smith if he could get him some pistols. He might have to postpone his fight with the Germans until the day after tomorrow.

The men all arrived back at about eight o'clock just in time for their pasta sauce and spaghetti. Caruso had bought four bottles of wine and everybody ate together. Sabini asked everybody to meet in the communal lounge. Bianchi had to wash up again because he was useless at selling raffle tickets.

Everybody congregated in the lounge.

Sabini began, "What we're going to do is to take out the Germans in Farringdon. They drink in the

Hoop and Grapes. What I want to know is how we are going to do it and what we are going to do after? I don't want bloodshed but if it's necessary it must be done."

Caruso said, "we could bring guns as a scare tactic. We might not even have to use them."

Sabini said, "After we win what are we going to do?"

Bastoni said, "What we'll do is kidnap the leader, bring him back here and thrash out a deal."

"Who's the leader?," said Caruso.

"Gerd," said Bastoni. "He is about six feet six," continued Bastoni.

Sabini was impressed with Bastoni's knowledge. Caruso got jealous.

Everybody agreed that they would bring guns and knives. The meeting went well. The only problem was what to do after the victory. Sabini would see Mr Smith tomorrow to ask how he could get firearms and the benevolent corrupt police to help him. The gang bought some more wine across the road at the off-licence. Bianchi got drunk. They all chatted about the Germans and went to sleep quite late.

Morning arrived in Soho. Everybody made their own breakfast. The smell of bacon permeated the three-story house. Sabini was up with Bastoni. They decided to have lunch with Mr Smith at The Dorchester in a few hour's time to try and get the guns for the German rendezvous. The rest were going to sell raffle tickets. This time in shops like Bastoni had done days earlier.

Lunchtime arrived and Sabini and Bastoni were seated at Mr Smith's table. In came Mr Smith who was delighted to see his protégé and his friend at the table. They all ordered pasta with cream, ham and peas and drank water.

"Mr Smith, we are going to expand and I need your help," said Sabini to Mr Smith.

"Carry on," said Mr Smith.

"We are looking to takeover Farringdon," said Sabini.

"Are the Germans not in the way?," asked Mr Smith.

"Yes," said Sabini. "We need some guns just to scare them," Sabini continued.

"We won't use them unless they fire at us," said Bastoni.

"When do you need them by?," asked Mr Smith.

"We need them now," said Sabini.

"Ok, what we will do is have a nice lunch, and then go by carriage to Islington to my friend's house."

Their pasta arrived and it was delicious.

In the carriage to Islington, Mr Smith talked about his racehorse that made him, how much money he made and continues to make whilst he was in stud.

"Why don't you buy one of his foals?," asked Bastoni to Mr Smith.

"I've got my foals in Sabini's organisation, you are my investment."

They had reached Pentonville and only had a mile or so left to the weapon place and ironmongers. Mr Smith would call him 'Billy Bullet'.

Mr Smith left the carriage, paid the fare and told Sabini and Bastoni to wait outside. The journey from The Dorchester took half an hour. Sabini and Bastoni decided they only needed four guns, as guns were unheard of in London - they mainly used knives.

Mr Smith came out and ushered in Sabini and Bastoni. Billy Bullet was a portly man who knew his stuff.

He asked, "how many do you need? And do you need repeat fire or single shot?"

Sabini asked, "How much are the single shots?"

"I have two pistols and two muskets," said Billy Bullet.

"Ok," said Sabini, "how much are they with forty bullets?"

"Billy Bullet replied, "Ten pounds... Can you show us how to operate them?"

"It's easy - you just press this latch button to unlock it, put in the bullet and close it. The top part has got a safety catch. It's the same with the musket," said Billy Bullet.

They purchased the guns and because Mr Smith didn't live far, he invited them to his big six-bedroom house in Islington. Sabini and Bastoni were happy to accompany him. They went inside the house. Bastoni made coffee and Sabini talked to Mr Smith about the Santaniello family that would help Mr Smith have company in his home and look after him. Sabini mentioned the fact that it will be this week. Mr Smith was delighted and knew that his hundred-pound investment in Sabini would reap more of a return than his racehorse. Plus he had to adopt an Italian family this week. Sabini would sort it out and he was growing into his role as an organised leader.

Sabini and Bastoni went to recruit more men in Clerkenwell for tonight's fight. They were successful especially as he offered a pound if they turned up. He recruited another fifteen. Sabini and Bastoni talked in the carriage back home about tonight's fight with the Germans over the spoils of Farringdon.

"We have to storm into the Hoops and Grapes waving guns, then we isolate the leader Gerd and take him home like a kidnap victim," said Sabini.

"What if none of them are there?," asked Bastoni.

"Then what we will do is send a forward patrol to the pub first and they can report back to us to see if it's on."

The carriage continued back through Pentonville and onto 27 Wardour Street. They had arrived home. Caruso and the others were there. The rest were doing well with the Soho raffle tickets. Bianchi was making the pasta sauce. He knew his role in the organisation. Sabini liked him. They had about six hours to go before the potential confrontation. They decided to play stud poker (only for pennies though because he wanted nobody in his organisation going skint).

Dinner was ready and it was pretty silent knowing the enormity of the night ahead. The Clerkenwell recruits arrived. The house was packed. Some of the new recruits had some food. There was a kind of silence but Bastoni kept the spirits alive.

Sabini was wondering which two of the gang would go into the Hoops and Grapes first and identify the leader there. There were thirty of them. Sabini delegated Rossi and Massi to go on forward patrol. The rest walked in pairs and threesomes, a couple of minutes behind each other. The organisation advanced well. It was nice and dark. They all accumulated around the corner from the park in a little bit of green space away from houses. Sabini sent Rossi and Massi into the pub.

Rossi and Massi were chosen because they didn't look Italian. They were fair-haired and looked more German than Italian. They looked around and could not but help notice that the leader Gerd was there with about eight or nine of his gang. Rossi and Massi finished their drink and walked out.

The pair then approached Sabini and told him that the leader was there. The gang loaded their guns and marched to the pub.

Gerd, the German, was holding court, boasting about how much money he had made this year. He was drunk on vodka. It was about half-past ten. His men were laughing at his jokes.

All of a sudden, in came the Sabini gang through the two entrances. They stormed into the Germans with good old-fashioned fisty cuffs. The leader Gerd was hard to pin down. He gave as good as he got. The other Germans were beaten but Gerd the leader wasn't.

Sabini got his pistol out and pointed it at Gerd. Then Bastoni got his pistol out and he too pointed it at the German leader.

The German put his hands up and said, "Don't shoot!"

"You're coming with us," said Sabini.

"Don't torture me otherwise you can shoot me now," said the German leader.

"Come on let's go," and it was all over within minutes.

Sabini was proud of his boys and the objective had been realised. The gang were paid a pound each. Bianchi never came because he had to wash up and make the beds. He never knew that an extra bed would be needed that night. Even Bianchi got a pound.

Sabini walked with Gerd at the front of the pack just in front of the three other gang members who had guns pointed at the German leader. They all got home at about midnight.

Rossi was given a gun and he was instructed to take the German leader to a bedroom and keep guard over him all night. The others played cards and discussed how they would carve up

Farringdon. Rossi got bored keeping guard over the German.

Sabini said, "Don't worry I will get someone else at four in the morning."

The card game was a bit of a joust between Bastoni and Massi. Massi had a feeling that Sabini would nominate him to take over the guard duty over the German. The card game finished and Bastoni won a sizeable amount.

Sabini then said the dreaded words to Massi, "Can you take over from Rossi?"

"No problem, Boss," said Massi.

And with that everybody went to sleep apart from Massi.

Chapter Six

German Roulette

"What the fuck do you want?," said Gerd to Sabini.

"Don't be like that otherwise I'll get you shot."

Sabini thought about a mock execution. He told Bastoni to guard Gerd whilst he went downstairs to arrange a mock execution. He told Caruso to have a false conversation with him outside the German's bedroom door. Within earshot of the German but out of sight, they walked upstairs and were on the landing within hearing distance of the German.

"Where shall we bury the body?," asked Sabini to Caruso.

"This is difficult we have to shoot him first but the gun will make a noise."

The German heard this and was trembling.

"We can shoot him, then put him in a blanket and bury him in the garden," said Caruso.

"Okay, we will do it tonight," said Sabini.

"Yes, we will put four bullets in his head," said Caruso. It was a slight exaggeration by Caruso.

Sabini said, "one will do".

The German heard the conversation and went white. Even Bastoni thought it was a real conversation.

Bastoni got bored guarding the German and asked Sabini for a handover. Sabini agreed and now it was Rossi's turn to guard the German. Bastoni wanted breakfast and a meeting with the gang about the day's plan. He spoke to Sabini about this and Sabini was only too happy about this.

"First thing is, Bianchi does the pasta sauce and gets the wine. I will give him the money. Massi is asleep he can guard the German at about seven o'clock. Massi will be on the night shift. Me, Bastoni and Caruso will rendezvous with Mr Smith. The rest of you can go to Faringdon and sound out the protection money market by selling raffle tickets just to understand how much they pay the Germans," said Sabini.

Rossi was told about the day's events by Bastoni and said "Shit, I'm here for hours guarding the German."

The German still thought he was getting killed that night. He said to Rossi "Am I getting killed tonight?"

Rossi said, "I don't know. Do you want something to eat?"

The German didn't know if he was hungry or not. Rossi shouted for Bianchi to come upstairs. Bianchi came upstairs and said to him to make bacon and eggs for Gerd the German. Within minutes the smell of bacon aroused the German's appetite. He ate his breakfast in ninety seconds - he thought it might be his last meal. He particularly liked the bread with olive oil.

The other ten members of the gang were not doing well, as the shopkeepers still thought that the Germans controlled the protection money in Farringdon. They then all got together, regrouped and found out that the Germans got three shillings a shop for a week and it was paid on a Saturday morning. That worked out as fifteen pounds a week. Saturday was a couple of days away. There were about a hundred businesses including seven hotels. They were told not to pay the Germans any more money. There were no Germans to be seen. They even sold raffle tickets.

It was now lunchtime and they went to a bakery. They told the baker not to pay for protection on Saturday. The baker gave them free sandwiches.

Sabini was in The Dorchester again with Caruso and Bastoni. They welcomed Mr Smith who had stopped buying *The Times*.

"First thing is first," began Sabini. "This is Caruso and this is Bastoni. Boys, this is Mr Smith. We have a family to help you at home. They're called the Santaniello family. The father works as a tiler. The mother keeps house and the kid is at school. They can move in as soon as you want."

"Splendid," said Mr Smith.

"I spoke to the chief police officer and he wants five pounds a week to turn a blind eye - even if you become really big."

Sabini thought about the Brighton races which were on Monday. He also thought about The Savoy Hotel and The Hilton for his next steps as putting in prostitutes. Caruso could have The Dorchester and Bastoni could have The Ritz. He would hold interviews for the role of pimp amongst the rest of his gang tomorrow.

They ordered razor clams, mussels and fried potatoes with creamed carrots and ice cream was served after. Mr Smith was insistent on paying the bill. The men then retired to the bar.

Mr Smith got on really well with Bastoni.

"Are you second-in-command, Bastoni?"

"I really don't know, Mr Smith."

Caruso was listening and became increasingly jealous. Mr Smith then asked Sabini who was second-in-command. Sabini answered that they were both joint second-in-command.

Mr Smith then got into the horse carriage for his trip back home to Islington. Sabini, Caruso and Bastoni decided to walk through Mayfair and Covent Garden. They talked about what they were going to do with the German, how they would collect the protection money from Farringdon and they sorted out The Savoy with more prostitutes. They arrived home to relieve Rossi of his guard duties. Rossi said that he'd fed him. But was due for lunch.

"Let him starve," said Caruso.

Sabini said to the German, "we have taken over Farringdon and the only problem we have is keeping you alive. Having you dead will help us."

The German was still quiet. At times he wished he was dead. But he didn't want to be buried in the garden covered with a sheet.

Sabini said to the German, "I will come back in an hour and I want you to tell me why I should keep you alive."

It was Massi's turn again to guard the German but Massi wanted to kill him.

The rest of the gang returned from Farringdon and briefed Sabini about how lucrative it was. It worked out at about fifteen pounds a week. Sabini then thought he was paying the prostitutes too much. He said to Caruso to renegotiate and half each would be fair.

Sabini then went upstairs to speak to the German who was beginning to feel like a condemned man.

"So tell me what can you offer," said Sabini. There was a bit of silence.

"All I have is Farringdon and about fifteen whores. I've worked hard for it. The Germans would change leaders every six months. I was their longest-serving leader. I'm in my fourth year, What I can do is make sure you get the protection money and I will give you the whores. I also want to work with you. You can make me second-in-command and I will be loyal. It's up to you how much you pay me. I have money for now," Sabini said. "I am going to keep you under guard until

Saturday, then I want the protection money from Farringdon and I might need the prostitutes for a later date."

With that Sabini left to join his gang downstairs. The German was saved for now.

Sabini went with Caruso and Bastoni. It was a good twenty-five minute walk to The Savoy from Soho. They had to pass through Leicester Square and then The Strand. They didn't know if The Savoy manager would be compliant with Sabini's idea to put Brass in The Savoy. When they arrived, the manager wasn't even there so they had to speak to the service manager.

"Where is the manager then?"

"He is not well," said the service manager.

"I run Soho and Farringdon and I can give you three hundred and sixty-five pounds a year just to have a few girls here. I already have girls in The Dorchester and The Ritz. The Savoy seems natural to be the same."

"What sort of girls?," said the service manager.

Caruso then got him by the throat and whispered "girls you cock."

"Ok, Ok," said the service manager.

"The password for the prostitutes is 'Sabini girls'. Make sure you tell the doorman."

They left The Savoy to make their way back home. Sabini decided when he got back to hold a vote to see who won the raffle of three pounds and thirty-six pence. He couldn't wait to go home to see the boys.

Massi switched the guarding duties with Rossi. Sabini got fourteen bits of paper and a pen. He decided that he wouldn't be in to vote to see who kept the raffle money. He gave a bit of paper to everyone and then collected the results. It was Bianchi who won by a landslide. It was the most he had ever had. He went red - flushed with happiness. At least he could play cards later after the dinner he was preparing. Sabini said to him not to play cards and also he could not participate in next week's draw, as he was the reigning winner. Bianchi was still happy.

Dinner was a happy affair - pasta with meatballs. They had even given the German upstairs some. Sabini thought about buying a long table with lots of chairs around it. At least the boys wouldn't have to eat on their laps and play cards on the floor.

Tomorrow would consist of selling raffle tickets in Soho, then Farringdon shops protection and hotels. Then he would meet Mr Smith for lunch. After he would interview the gang for the position of the pimp at The Savoy. Caruso had The Dorchester and Bastoni had The Ritz. The job at The Savoy was up for grabs.

The gang were finishing off their wine and finishing off their card game. It was time for bed.

Friday morning arrived and everybody got up together. Bianchi made breakfast again. The boys came downstairs and sat in the lounge. Marchisio was in charge of guarding the German. Machisio and the German had breakfast together. This time everybody had herrings and eggs with bread and olive oil. Marchisio didn't even know how to load the gun. It was pre-loaded so that was alright.

Sabini brought nine of the lads to the second-hand furniture shop to buy a long table and sixteen chairs. They only had to walk around the corner. Bastoni stayed at home with Caruso, Marchisio and Bianchi.

Sabini said to the lads, "What do you reckon to the mahogany one?"

"It's nice," said the lads. There were also enough chairs.

Sabini asked the shopkeeper, "how much for the chairs?"

The shopkeeper said, "three pounds."

Sabini said, "I will give you two and a half pounds and we will carry them out of the shop, what do you say?"

"That will be fine, sir."

Sabini gave him three pounds and the shopkeeper gave him a ten shilling note change. The Sabini gang hated the pennies that had accrued from the raffle and had to find a way to change them into notes. They would buy wine, pasta meat and clothes which would be used in the guard games.

The table and chairs had arrived and Sabini gave the rest of the day off to the gang but reminded them about the pimp's interview at 3:30 pm. Somebody took over Marchisio's guard duties for the German. Sabini told Bianchi not to get involved with the card game and told Caruso to find fifteen hookers for The Dorchester, The Ritz and The Savoy.

It was going to be a busy day. He paid everybody in pennies. Two hundred and forty each. He paid Caruso and Bastoni in notes. They didn't shake hands when they walked.

It was an unwritten agreement that Sabini would meet Mr Smith every day at twelve o'clock at The

Dorchester. Mr Smith could not be happier mixing business with pleasure. He would leave his Islington home at eleven thirty and arrive at The Dorchester at just after twelve.

Sabini and Bastoni also arrived at just after twelve. They had a glass of red and bought Mr Scotch his usual Scotch.

"Why don't you take Holborn?," said Mr Smith.

"We can't take Holborn because it's yours," said Sabini.

"It's not mine because I've only got twenty-one houses there are three gangs there, the Irish, the

Scottish and the Welsh. They're all fighting each other for the spoils of crime. The Irish gang leader has got sixty-seven houses. The Scottish leader has forty-nine, the Welsh leader has got thirty-seven. The hotels have shut down so there are no ladies of the night and no raffle tickets being sold. There are a few pubs open."

There was a weird peace like a calm before the storm.

"I want you to be the storm, Charley," said Mr Smith to the Italian gang leader.

"Who's on top at the moment, Mr Smith?"

"I think the Irish are, they are also holding on to Kilburn and Maida Vale, so they can't spare the men. They've gotten too big too quickly. I'm lucky to have you boys in Soho. I think we are the only area that's peaceful and safe."

They ordered asparagus with fricassee chicken and garlic croutons.

Bastoni said, "I've got the idea for how to deal with The Holborn problem. We link up with the Scottish and the Welsh and take over the Irish. We give the Scottish and the Welsh a third each and we keep a third. The Irish get kicked back to Kilburn and Maida Vale."

Mr Smith and Sabini thought it was a great idea and would organise a meeting with the Scots and the Welsh. Holborn was a good couple of miles away. Again they retired to The Dorchester Bar where Sabini asked Mr Smith if he wanted to be on the panel of the pimp interview. Mr Smith politely declined. They had their drinks and left.

"Don't forget Brighton Racecourse on Monday," said Mr Smith.

"We won't," said Sabini and Bastoni.

The walk back was not too long. Sabini told Bastoni that Caruso was the pimp in The Dorchester and that Bastoni would be the pimp at

The Ritz. Bastoni was over the moon and joked that Sabini would have to interview him. They arrived home and Bianchi was making a five-hour sauce. Caruso came in and said he had secured fifteen girls for the three hotels: The Dorchester, The Ritz and The Savoy.

"Right lads, it's interview time to become a pimp at The Savoy, you will all be interviewed in the lounge. Me, Caruso and Bastoni will be on the panel. We will make our decision tonight after our pasta."

They would go in alphabetical order. They called in Bianchi who shouted out to the others - "Make sure you stir the sauce!" Bianchi sat down.

Sabini asked, "what makes you a good pimp?"

"Because I make a good sauce and even prostitutes have to eat."

"Thank you, Bianchi that's enough, send in Carlucci."

Carlucci came in and Sabini asked again, "What makes a good pimp?"

"A good pimp is loyal to the organisation, fifty per cent of the money goes to the organisation and fifty per cent goes to the girls. It's important that everyone is happy and organised. I won't fall in love."

"That will do," said Sabini.

He interviewed the rest of them. They just couldn't match the class of Carlucci. The German was being guarded by Rossi and Massi. Sabini came upstairs.

"Hello Charley," said the German to Sabini.

"Hello Gerd, do you fancy any dinner and some wine?"

Sabini sent Rossi to get six bottles of wine. It came in a crate of six.

"Do you know what you want to do with your life, being that you still have one?," said Sabini.

"Protection money, whores and a good wage and loyalty goes without doubt. Am I in?," asked Gerd the German.

"I won't give you a wage, I will give you ten per cent of the protection money. You might have to give me the whores and I will give you ten per cent of the raffle money. Now come downstairs and meet the gang."

The German came downstairs slowly. He still thought the guns were pointing at him.

He said, "yo, Sabini where he should sit?"

"On the couch," said Sabini.

The pasta was served. The German enjoyed his wine and asked Sabini if he could buy another six bottles. Sabini said "Ok" but said that Caruso and Bastoni were on pimp duty. He also revealed that "Carlucci was the winner of the pimp job at the Savoy." The three would be starting work soon.

Everybody was eating. Gerd got chatting to everyone. He quite liked it (now that he knew that he wasn't getting shot). Gerd eventually met everyone and he appeared to get on well with them all. He was looking for a game of poker. Rossi came back with six more bottles of wine. Caruso, Bastoni and Carlucci left for their pimping jobs.

The cards came out and stud poker was the game. Gerd won the first two games. Sabini thought about strolling down to The Savoy to see how Carlucci was getting along. In he came and spotted Carlucci. It was quite busy. It was only ten o'clock and the five girls were doing well.

"How you doing?," said Sabini to Carlucci.

"Yes, good everything is going fine, we've made six pounds already. That's three for the girls and three for you".

"That's not for me, that's for the organisation," said Sabini.

"Well I know it's for the organisation. You know what I mean."

"Yes, I do know what you mean."

One of the girls came up and asked if Sabini wanted to do business.

Carlucci said, "This is Sabini your manager."

"What the same Sabini we have to use as a password to get into the Savoy?"

"Yes," said Carlucci.

"My name is Alice."

"Obviously my name is Sabini, do you want a drink?," asked Sabini.

"Yes I will have a gin and Schweppes," said Alice. She quite fancied Sabini.

Meanwhile back in Soho, Gerd was cleaning up in poker and to endear himself, he even thought about giving the gang their money back. Bianchi still wanted to play but they refused his pleas. Gerd thought it would be a good idea to give Bianchi the profit he had made and withdraw from the game. The boys agreed. Bianchi loved it and loved Gerd as well. Things were going well for everybody. Bianchi lost everything in twenty minutes. Gerd didn't want to join the game. He acted like a gentleman and the boys loved him.

Back in The Savoy, Sabini was about to leave. Alice would miss him. Sabini didn't know this. He got a horse and carriage to the Ritz. The coachman was happy because he could get more clients from The Ritz - it was only two miles away. Sabini got in and again the Friday evening was balmy.

Tomorrow was a big day. It was all about Farringdon.

Sabini waltzed into The Ritz and it took him a little while to find Bastoni. It was packed. There were no girls. That's because the girls were busy upstairs.

"Ciao Bastoni, where are the girls?"

"They've been busy as fuck – literally." Sabini liked that joke.

"Do you want a drink?," said Bastoni.

"I'll have a glass of red wine," said Sabini. One of the girls came over.

They were charging a special rate of ten shillings. The girl that came over was called Elizabeth. She was just as attractive as Alice in The Savoy...

"You're Sabini aren't you? You are so handsome," said Elizabeth.

"Thank you," said Sabini.

They chatted for a little while and another one of the girls came over. Sabini asked Bastoni how much he had made.

"Three and a half pounds," said Bastoni.

"That's impressive," said Sabini.

There were still hours to go and The Ritz was doing well. If the girls were asked to stay the night, the men would have to pay upfront, that way the organisation could go home at about three and got the money early for the overnight stays. The total for The Ritz had climbed to five and a half pounds.

The Ritz manager came over and bought Sabini and Bastoni a drink. He didn't have to pay for it because he was the manager. The atmosphere that night in The Ritz was electric .

Sabini walked a short distance to The Dorchester. He gave the doorman a shilling. The doorman said, "They're all in there. It's very busy in there." Sabini found Caruso easily. Caruso always sat at the bar in the same place. Julia had been the busiest girl - she always was. She would wash her private parts often. All the major hotels provided soap and clean towels.

"Ciao Caruso."

"Ciao Boss," said Caruso.

"How is it going?," said Sabini.

"We are cleaning up."

Julia came over smelling of soap. Sabini talked to Julia. Caruso got jealous. Sabini talked to Julia about opening a brothel in Soho.

Julia said, "Can I be madam?"

"No you can't," said Sabini.

"You're too important here."

"Can I find you a madam then? I heard that Farringdon is going through a bit of a crisis."

Sabini knew why because he had just taken it. He asked Caruso how much he had taken. He said four pounds. The Dorchester manager arrived and Sabini gave him a pound. Caruso had told the girls earlier that it was a fifty-fifty split where the girls were concerned.

Back to the card game, Rossi got an amazing run of games. He was the only one who didn't drink. The rest were very tipsy and started arguing. Rossi won two and a half pounds and his pennies weighed quite heavily.

Sabini thought about going home and wanted to make sure the boys got a good night's sleep. It was only a relatively short walk. He told Caruso that he was going. Julia had found another gentleman.

The other girls were all busy. Sabini had noticed that some of the men had cocaine residue around their noses. It was probable that his girls were on it as well. He said goodbye to the doorman and wandered home. He then thought about a party in Soho on Wednesday with all fifteen girls, as well as gin, wine and white snuff.

When he arrived home there was eleven of them and Gerd the German. Sabini asked Rossi what the German was like. Rossi said, "The German won a lot of money off us, then gave his winnings to Bianchi who lost it all. He was a gentleman."

Some of them had gone to bed. Bianchi was embarrassed that he'd lost Gerd's money. He said to Rossi to wake the others up for tomorrow's plan.

The other three came downstairs and Sabini asked Gerd to speak first.

"What we do is you lot follow me. That's it."

"What if the other Germans turn up wanting their money?"

"Leave it to me. We have guns. We can also sell raffle tickets." "Did you hear that boys? Tomorrow Gerd is in charge. I will give you twenty per cent of the protection money," said Sabini to Gerd.

"That's more than I got before I was kidnapped," said Gerd.

There was no wine left. Everybody went to bed. Gerd was in. It was one in the morning. They would have to go through Holborn. Sabini wanted a nice early start.

Chapter Seven

Farringdon, Poker and More

Bianchi woke up first and got the bacon on. Bianchi thought it was more of an English breakfast. An Italian breakfast was cake and coffee. Anyway, one by one, they came downstairs. Bianchi was kind of upset because he was running out of olive oil. Someone would have to go to Clerkenwell to get it. It was okay though as it was close to Faringdon.

Sabini came downstairs. The smell was lovely.

Bianchi said to Sabini, "Can you get us some olive oil from Clerkenwell, please Boss?"

"No problem, I will get Massi on the case."

Massi overheard and thought 'Why me?' Everybody was up. Except for Caruso. Bastoni and Carlucci who had got home at about five in the morning. They left the thirty-odd pounds in Sabini's room.

Sabini said, "Everybody stay close to Gerd. Especially when we walk through Holborn. There's a good chance the Scottish, the Irish and the Welsh will still be in bed."

It was only half-past eight. Most of the shops didn't open until nine. It took about half an hour by foot so the timings were perfect.

They walked at a steady pace and breezed through Holborn. There were a lot of shops in the high street.

"We are going to clean up today and fill our pockets, I just know it - they won't know a thing," said Rossi.

"That's right they won't know what hit them, it's the first time I've walked with more than eight people. I feel honoured to walk with this organisation. Really I do. All of the shops are on the high street, just follow me. The rest of the German gang won't surface until eleven o'clock. We'll be long gone," said Gerd.

"I've got to meet Mr Smith at The Dorchester. Can you get a horse and carriage in Farringdon?," said Sabini to Gerd.

"Difficult," said Gerd, we'll be back in Soho by half-eleven, no problem. I will even carry you, Charley. Sabini didn't know if he liked being called Charley or Sabini.

They arrived and the first shop was the butchers. They all got in the shop and the butcher said "Good morning" to the gang and handed over three shillings. Sabini then bought twenty sausages for two shillings and got Massi to carry them. They walked next door to the greengrocer and again it was easy. The greengrocer handed over another three shillings. This time Sabini bought some cabbage and gave them to Rossi to carry. This carried on all morning. They even collected money from the Hoop and Grapes and sold quite a few raffle tickets on sale or return.

They collected from fifty-five shops as some were closed. Three shillings a shop. That was just over eight pounds. Then they were finished. Gerd had spotted a couple of Germans milling around. He told Sabini that they were no threat and they would have reported it to their friends that Gerd was a turncoat.

Sabini loved the fact that they had finished. He wanted to meet Mr Smith about how they would carve up Holborn. He also liked the fact that they were making money. They all walked back through Holborn again. Everybody was in fine form except Massi and Rossi who had to carry the sausages and cabbages back. Sabini gave Gerd one and a half pounds. Sabini walked to The Dorchester. The rest of the gang walked home.

Sabini had about seventy pounds but he owed Mr Smith a hundred pounds. He walked into

The Dorchester with the intention of paying Mr Smith at least fifty pounds off the total. When he did Mr Smith said, "What's this?" Sabini explained that he had had a good twenty-four hours. Mr Smith said, "it's okay, you don't have to pay me for months."

Mr Smith then explained that he had met the leader of the Scottish and the leader of the Welsh. He had organised a meeting on Tuesday in The Dorchester the day after the Brighton races.

Sabini loved Mr Smith. They then ordered a Spanish paella with seafood - it went down a treat! They talked about Brighton and Holborn. Sabini also needed another house in Soho for his brothel.

Mr Smith said "no problem." Sabini would have to ask either Caruso or Gerd if they could get a madam.

They finished their lunch and again retired to the bar. Massi fancied sausages and cabbage for dinner and forgot about the olive oil he was supposed to have got for Bianchi. He would put someone in a carriage and go to Clerkenwell in the morning.

Sabini walked home and had a lot on his mind. He was thinking about the Scottish and the Welsh and he thought about getting a madam. He thought about the Brighton races but he thought the most important thing was the olive oil he needed. He really should have shared a carriage to Islington with Mr Smith and then stopped at Clerkenwell to get the oil and come back to Soho. He gave himself a rollicking for not doing it.

When he got home he decided to pay everybody. He gave everybody a pound. Most of them were all playing poker. They had got some wine and were drinking at a leisurely pace.

Sabini went up to Bianchi and told him to make sausages and cabbage for dinner. Sabini then went upstairs for a nap. The card game ended up pretty even, only Rossi lost.

"How come I lost?," said Rossi.

"I got some good cards as well," Massi said.

"The reason why you lost is because when you got the best hand nobody got a good hand to go with you."

The boys carried on playing. Gerd won again. He would ask Sabini later if he wanted to open up a card school in Soho and it would make them money.

Caruso, Bastoni and Carlucci were about to get up after Friday's night shift at the major hotels. They were tired but happy. Bianchi made them the usual

English breakfast at lunchtime but there was no olive oil.

Sabini could hear the noises and got up as well. He asked two members of the organisation if they could get a horse and carriage from The Dorchester and go to Clerkenwell and pick up jars of tomatoes, olive oil, dried pasta and fresh pasta. Also to pick up a joint of beef, broccoli and potatoes and anything else they thought they needed. A pound would be enough but he gave them one pound and ten shillings. There were sixteen to feed. Clerkenwell was the best place in London to buy Italian food. The two men that went to Clerkenwell would tell the coachman to wait whilst they shopped.

The Italians moved into Clerkenwell in the 1850s and 1860s. They were the first generation. Their sons and daughters spoke English as their first language and they could also communicate in the same kind of dialect Italian that the organisation could, but they were far more conversant in English.

Nobody ever collected protection money in Clerkenwell or Soho. This was due to the Italians sticking together in Clerkenwell and Mr Smith in Soho. Protection was paid in the rest of London but there were a lot grey areas and many disputes and fights. Some areas like Islington and the Strand (where The Savoy was) were up for grabs.

The coachman waited for the boys to do their shopping in Clerkenwell. They even bought onions, garlic bay leaves and fresh parsley. They got home and had spent two shillings short of a pound. They gave Sabini twelve shillings change. Sabini gave them a shilling each for going. It was Sunday and tomorrow was a big day at Brighton.

Caruso said to Sabini that they had done well last night and Bastoni and Carlucci said the same.

"How do you think tonight will go?," said Sabini about having the girls in the hotels.

"We should be okay," said Bastoni.

"I'm not so sure," said Carlucci.

Caruso said, "it is what it is."

"Did you know we are going to Brighton Races tomorrow?," said Sabini.

"Do you want us to come?," said Caruso... "We can be back for two o'clock in the morning, I trust my girls with the takings," added Caruso.

"I trust my girls as well," said Bastoni and Carlucci.

"Ok," said Sabini.

"We will have breakfast together and then get the train from Victoria to Brighton at about eleven in the morning. I think the first race at Brighton is at two o'clock. The last race is at 4:30 pm."

It was about seven o'clock and Caruso, Bastoni and Carlucci, went to their respective hotels - The Dorchester, The Ritz and The Savoy.

Sabini fancied a game of poker. He had heard that the German was a brilliant poker player and was looking for a one to one showdown with him. The card game started at about four in the afternoon. There was Sabini, Gerd, Caruso, Carlucci, Bastoni, Rossi and Massi and one other. The first hand was dealt. Bastoni won it with three fours. There was a lot of chinking of penny coins. To win a pound you had to win two hundred and forty pennies. There was hardly any silver used; it wasn't high stakes.

Bastoni again mentioned that the organisation should have a card school with a croupier dealing where we could also offer drinks and sandwiches. Sabini liked the idea and would look into it as well as a brothel.

Sabini had a flush. Massi had three twos. Sabini raised. Massi re-raised. Sabini raised again. It wasn't a bad pot. They saw each other. Sabini won the equivalent of six shillings. Sabini was happy.

Massi wasn't because he had lost all his money. He asked Bianchi if he could borrow some but Bianchi said no. Bianchi was happy that he was going to Brighton tomorrow. He still had all of his raffle money.

The richest was Sabini, followed by the German, Caruso, Bastoni, Carlucci, Rossi and then Bianchi. The others were all the same apart from Massi who was totally skint. Then they ate their sausages and cabbage.

"Can we get another two houses in Soho," asked Bastoni.

"One for the brothel and one for the card school?"

"Yes we can, I will ask Mr Smith," said Sabini.

The game continued and the much-anticipated showdown between the German and Sabini was realised. It was quite a big pot. The German had three jacks and Sabini had three queens. Sabini gave his winnings to Massi. Massi was so happy to rejoin the game. He promised Sabini he would keep the train fayre for Brighton.

Caruso walked into The Dorchester where some of the girls were. The other two walked in soon after (there were five in total) - the same amount that were in The Ritz and The Savoy.

Caruso liked Julia. He wished she wasn't a prostitute. He bought her the usual drink and he bought the others the same drink - gin and Schweppes. He had a glass of red wine. He asked Julia what she would do if she wasn't doing this.

"I would make dresses, I would. I make dresses for myself as well."

"Can you make suits for us?," said Caruso.

"Course I can," said Julia.

A gentleman came over he was becoming quite regular as a client. They got a room and away they went.

The Ritz was busy and you would not think it was a Sunday night. Bastoni was at the bar and he saw a lot of men with white powder near their nostrils. He was fascinated by this. It was sold to be an anaesthetic. It took the pain away apparently. He heard that some would put it in some water and dab their eyes to alleviate the pain. He just wanted to do it like you did snuff. He asked Elizabeth one of the girls to get him some.

She said, "If you do it too late you won't sleep."

Bastoni said, "When I leave at two, I want you to look after the money. Is that okay?"

"Yes, that's fine," she said and off she went to get some cocaine for Bastoni.

At The Savoy, Carlucci was in fine form. One of his girls had just come back from being upstairs and another one had just gone upstairs with a gentleman. He also wondered why some of the men had white powder showing in their nostrils. He was holding court in the Savoy.

"Do you want a drink?," said one of the girls.

"Yes I will have a glass of red," said Carlucci.

Carlucci then asked what she did in the week when she wasn't working.

"Oh I look after my mum," she replied. "She is pretty poorly so all I do is feed her and give her cocaine."

"What? You give her cocaine?"

"Yes, it's really good for her ailments," she replied. "I've got some if you want?"

The Dorchester was quiet again. Julia was the only one doing regular business. Caruso seemed a bit bored. But he knew this was the life of a pimp. He was on his third glass of red. Julia came back and Caruso asked Julia if she knew a madam that could take over the brothel they were opening soon in Soho.

"I know someone, Madelain the madam, she is experienced and all the girls love her."

"Can we meet next week?," said Caruso.

"Yeah, no problem," said Julia.

"I will give you the address and you can come round to the house in Soho," said Caruso.

"Ok, deal done," said Julia.

Elizabeth got some cocaine for Bastoni. Bastoni asked how he should do it.

"The same way you do snuff," Elizabeth said.

Bastoni said, "That's easy."

He took some and immediately walked up to a stranger talking to another girl at a table. He went over and talked to her for seven minutes non-stop. He then introduced himself as 'Cirio Bastoni'. The girls thought he said 'cheerio'. They said 'cheerio too'. The girls could have been titled ladies.

Then Bastoni spoke to another stranger at the bar. Another girl. This time he gave her a chance to speak.

"Hello, my gorgeous, how are you? My name is Cirio Bastoni."

"My name is Kate. What do you do Cirio?"

"I look after girls and make sure they don't get beaten up."

So you're a pimp then," said Kate.

"I'm not exactly a pimp. Because I don't work as a pimp every day. The other days I play cards I am a professional," said Bastoni.

"Do you fancy a game of cards?," said Kate.

"Only if it's poker."

Two of Bastoni's girls turned up from being upstairs to watch the game. Bastoni got thrashed because he would go in heavily without a hand. Kate used to play poker with her family at Christmas and Easter and was quite experienced. Bastoni lost about two quid. But he made Kate buy the drinks for him and the girls who always had gin and Schweppes.

The girl returned to Carlucci with the cocaine.

Carlucci said, "it won't kill me, will it?"

"No, it will be fine," said the girl.

"I normally put snuff on the back of my hand," said Carlucci.

"Do it that way," said the girl.

Carlucci did it, and said, "What's supposed to happen?"

Carlucci started feeling euphoric and invincible. He could not believe that he was with five pretty girls in The Ritz on cocaine. He started chatting to the barman - something he hadn't done before. He was happy. He caught the eye of a girl looking at him and went over and introduced himself. He bought her a sherry and he had red wine. He then went back to the bar on his stool. Then some of the girls came over and gave him the takings. Carlucci split the takings in half and gave half to the girls. He said he had to leave and told the girls to be fair when splitting the money in his absence. He got a horse and carriage to Soho.

Bastoni didn't want to go. He was too happy. The last thing he wanted to do was sleep. He tried to get drunk on red wine but couldn't.

Caruso was talking to Julia in The Dorchester. He enquired about opening up a tailor and dressmaker. Julia seemed interested. She could find enough staff and clients to make it pay.

Julia then said, "I could do both jobs. I want to be one of your girls forever and then become a madam."

"Shall I try and sort it out for you?," said Caruso.

"Please," said Julia.

With that Caruso took half the takings and gave the rest to the girls.

"Don't worry we will give you the rest of the money next time I see you," said Julia.

Caruso walked home.

Bastoni thought that he could go round the clock. He was absolutely flying. He went back to Kate at the bar and they chatted. Bastoni bought some drinks. He didn't know if he should have some more cocaine. He decided against it and was now feeling that it was best if he went home. He gave half the takings to the girls and made them promise to give the rest of the money when they saw each other next.

Chapter Eight

Brighton Races

Monday morning arrived and Bianchi was up early making breakfast. There was no shortage of olive oil. But he thought there might be a bread shortage. He stopped cooking and bought two loaves from around the corner. He then came back and resumed cooking the usual bacon and eggs.

Rossi and Massi came down first. It was good coming down early, as you were guaranteed a place at the table. The waft of fried bacon went through the house. Bianchi was good at making breakfast. Sabini would come down next with some of the gang. Bianchi would always give Sabini extra bacon. The German came downstairs and said "Buon Giorno." The rest said "Buon Giorno" too.

The others all came downstairs but there were not enough chairs. The German started talking about the quality of the food he was enjoying. Bianchi asked the German about the quality of food in the German gang.

"It was shit," said the German... "Porridge and cold sandwiches."

Caruso spoke to Sabini about the idea of a suit maker and dressmaker. Sabini liked it. It could be next to the brothel in Soho. They would moot the idea to Mr Smith on Tuesday. On Wednesday they had a meeting with the Holborn leaders, the Scottish leader and the Welsh leader. Everyone finished their breakfast and Sabini got Massi to do the washing up - Massi always ended up doing the menial jobs!

It was time to go to Victoria train station. Everybody was ready. There were sixteen of them. All dressed up. It was a good forty-five minute walk to Victoria train station. Sabini promised if it went well he would buy everybody new shoes. He put Gerd the German in front. Sabini was at the back. Bianchi was in the middle. They went through The Strand. Sabini wondered if there was potential in The Strand. Nobody knew, which meant that it was a possibility. They arrived at Victoria Station.

Sabini had also bought the four guns but no bullets. Sabini bought sixteen one day returns. It cost eight shillings. They all boarded.

Along the way, they marvelled at the spectacular scenery. Especially the rolling hills of the downs. They all agreed if they worked hard they would live in Sussex. They played and joked on the train. Bianchi held court. He was one of many that had never been on a train.

The train took a couple of hours. Bastoni and Carlucci were tired after last night's coke events. They never told anyone about it. They didn't even tell each other. The train stopped and they were looking forward to beating up the bookies.

When they got out there were many horse and carriages. Sabini got four carriages for the gang to Brighton Racecourse. It was a good mile and a half. When they got there it was fairly empty. The gang went to the bar and had a drink. The red wine was a lot cheaper than the one at The Dorchester, The Ritz and The Savoy.

Sabini said "no more drink" and they went for a walk. They saw the horses in the stables and

Bianchi said "if I get enough money I'm going to get one". They asked the groundsman if they could cross the racecourse to the other side. The groundsman said "no problem".

They were waiting for the bookies to arrive. They saw a couple of bookies set up their pitch. Sabini told the gang to walk back in fours to the bar. Brighton Racecourse was filling up with well-heeled gentlemen and posh ladies. Bastoni and Carlucci wished they had some cocaine. Sabini noticed this and told them to wait at the bar. Sabini then gave a bulletless gun each to the German, to Rossi and Massi. Sabini kept the last one to himself. It was half-past one and he was ready to strike.

He got the German to go over to the first bookmaker.

The German said to him, "I want fifty per cent of your profit, otherwise, I will smash your blackboard and pitch up."

The bookie (Mr Steinburger) said, "I can't do that, I don't earn enough money."

The German then got his gun out and discreetly pointed it at Steinburger.

The German said to Steinburger, "don't let me do this or I will kill you."

Steinburger said, "I will give you thirty per cent."

"You're lucky I'm not charging you sixty per cent. I will kill you after the racing has finished. I will get a carriage with you, shoot you then dump you out of the carriage."

"Ok, ok. I will give you the money," said Steinburger who then said, "I don't win every day."

Massi and Rossi worked together on the next two bookies playing Mr Nice and Mr Bad. Sabini thought it was good. It was the same Mr Nice and Mr Bad tactic Sabini had used himself when they kidnapped the German. Ten minutes later, the extortion was complete on all eight bookmakers.

"I will check all of your books to see you are not cheating us," Sabini said to the bookies.

There was a lot of money about. The gentlemen seemed rich and there were lots of them. They would all stay in Brighton hotels. He even saw one gentleman put a bunch of tenners on a horse. It must have been about fifty pounds. Sabini asked what horse the gentleman had backed. The bookie said "Garrido the favourite." The horse lost by a distance. Sabini and the gang were happy. The gang would be interested in horses that could possibly be a liability to their takings. Bastoni had noticed a lot of second favourites had won. It was a good day for the bookies.

The favourites had a bad day. They would leave before the last race as they didn't want to draw attention to themselves by collecting money. After the second last race, they collected in all six hundred and fifty-six pounds and eleven shillings. It was the most anybody had ever seen. Even the German had not seen that amount of money.

They went into the crowd and towards the carriages. They got into four of them and were taken to the train station. The train was only a minute away from departing. As they boarded,

Sabini grasped the money in his jacket pocket to make sure he didn't lose it.

Sabini wondered how he should share the money. He had to give ten per cent or sixty-five pounds to Mr Smith. He would also give twenty pounds each to the boys. That would leave about two hundred and eighty-five pounds. House prices were going up. They had been going up since the 1850s but they were due to come down (he would ask Mr Smith).

The train arrived at Victoria. They got into the horse and carriages and made their way to an Italian restaurant near Soho. The gang had never been so happy. They all ordered fine food and eight bottles of wine. Some of the lads wanted to go home early to play cards. Sabini forbade this for now as he didn't want anybody going skint tonight.

Everybody was going on about how brilliant the German was at Brighton Racecourse. They all had their dinner, drank some wine and then went home. Sabini said that they could play cards but with limited stakes. Once you lost your limited stakes, you were out. Sabini also said that tomorrow they would have to get their own shoes because he would give them twenty pounds each for today. He would also open up a brothel, a suit and a dressmaker.

The German won again at poker. So did Rossi too. The rest lost a little bit. They toyed with the idea of buying wine but decided not to. Sabini had a great day lined up. He would pay Mr Smith his ten per cent. He would also get Caruso to bring Julia to the house about the suit making and dressmaking. He needed a shop. He would also need another house for his brothel. It was a good day for the gang. They all went to bed at about twelve.

Chapter Nine

Buying Shoes

The smell of bacon again greeted the other's good morning. Bianchi was in a great mood. That's because he didn't have to go raffle ticket selling in Farringdon. One by one, the boys woke up. Two rashers of bacon and two eggs were served with some bread and olive oil. This was the norm every morning. Sausages took too long to cook.

Sabini had his breakfast and suggested shoe buying to the organisation, then Farringdon for raffle ticket selling. He asked Caruso, Bastoni and

Carlucci to stay behind. They could buy their shoes later.

"We have to collect the rest of the takings from Sunday night," said Sabini to Caruso, Bastoni and Carlucci.

"I also have to move the Santaniello family into Mr Smith's house in Islington," said Sabini.

It was nearing noon and the boys left home to see Mr Smith. They arrived at The Dorchester. Everybody said hello Mr Smith. Sabini gave the manager three pounds for the girls being allowed into The Dorchester for Friday, Saturday and Sunday. Sabini also said that after the meeting with Mr Smith, Caruso, Bastoni and Carlucci they would have to collect the money from the takings from the Ritz, The Dorchester and the Savoy.

Sabini said to Mr Smith that he needed three house keys for the Santaniello family to move in on Wednesday night. Mr Smith agreed. Sabini then gave sixty-five pounds to Mr Smith. Mr Smith couldn't believe how much it was. Sabini then gave him a hundred pounds, which is what he owed him for the loan. They had a good lunch of quails eggs with a salad of white onions and tomatoes. Mr Smith insisted on paying for it. It came to one pound and four shillings. Then they retired to the bar.

"I need a house and a shop in Soho," said Sabini.

Mr Smith said, "when do you need it by?"

"As soon as possible," said Sabini.

"We are going to open up a tailors and a dressmakers. The house will be for the ladies of the night," said Sabini.

Mr Smith said, "if I give you free rent I would want ten per cent."

Sabini did not like it, but he could not complain as if it wasn't for Mr Smith he would still be a waiter so it was still a win-win situation.

Mr Smith would see that he got three house keys and find out which house and premises he could help Sabini with. He then got into a horse and carriage and went home to Islington. He would pass St Pancras and Pentonville. He had also planned a meeting with the Scots and the Welsh the next day.

Sabini then said goodbye to Caruso, Bastoni and Carlucci as they had to meet up with the girls to get payment. Carlucci got a horse and carriage to The Savoy which was quite far away.

Sabini got home and found Bianchi making meatballs with beef and pork. He also used the breadcrumbs, white onions, garlic and parsley that was still there. Sabini marvelled at Bianchi's skill at rolling the mixture. He had to make thirty-two meatballs which worked out at two each for the gang.

Bianchi liked Sabini as well. What Bianchi said was that everybody had to put one shilling each and take it in turns to go to Clerkenwell to do the shopping. Sabini helped Bianchi roll the meatball then he had to go to Clerkenwell to tell the Santaniellos that they were moving out tomorrow to look after Mr Smith.

Sabini stopped a carriage and was taken to the house of Santaniello. He could have taken the fledgling tube. But it was complicated with lots of walking. He arrived at the house. He said to Mr Santaniello to meet him at The Dorchester at twelve with his wife and kid. He gave him three shillings for the expenses. Mr and Mrs Santaniello were overjoyed. Sabini then went shopping in Clerkenwell and bought ten jars of tomatoes and six packets of spaghetti for Bianchi's meatball sauce.

The boys had returned from selling raffle tickets they had done well. Bastoni, Caruso and Carlucci were still out there and not at home. Sabini got home and asked how it went. It went well with three pounds worth of tickets sold. Caruso turned up shortly after with four pounds. Bastoni took the takings at The Ritz - five pounds. A short while after, Carlucci turned up with six pounds.

Sabini gave the jars of tomatoes and spaghetti to Bianchi. He mixed it with the meatballs for a two-hour sauce. As usual, everybody complimented Bianchi. They ate two hours later. Sabini sent Massi to get the wine from the off-licence.

After dinner, the cards came out. Sabini said no shillings or notes. This time Bianchi was allowed to play. The German won again. Sabini also played and didn't play too badly. Bastoni won as well. The rest of the gang either broke even or lost. Everybody went to bed at about one in the morning. Sabini was looking forward to tomorrow. He also had the meeting with the Scottish leader Stuart and the Welsh leader Taffy at three o'clock in The Dorchester according to Mr Smith.

Sabini gave everybody the day off. They never bought shoes yesterday. It was time that everybody bought shoes. Sabini bought some shoes and the rest all bought leather black shoes. He thought also about the fact that when he bought his tailors and dressmaker, the gang could all buy suits from his shop at a discount price. There were sixteen of them in a shoe shop. It was amazing that the shoe shop owner had enough for six pairs. He would have to make the rest of them.

Sabini walked alone to The Dorchester. He always arrived early – Mr Smith liked that.

"Have you found me two high-ranking policemen from the Metropolitan Police?," said Sabini.

Mr Smith replied, "Yes I have, you can meet them on Saturday."

"Sounds great," said Sabini.

They ordered roast beef, roast potatoes and vegetables and both ordered Scotch. They always ordered the same meal. They never organised any of their meetings, they just happened naturally.

They retired to the bar. "We made a lot of money at Brighton," said Sabini.

"Yes, you did, you will have to go to Sandown, it is on next Tuesday."

Sabini was excited about Sandown. He thought it would be the making of the gang.

At three o'clock, the Scottish leader Stuart and the Welsh leader Taff came in. They introduced themselves. Mr Smith asked them if they wanted a drink. They both said scotch. It was a good sign that they were drinking the same drink. They all went to a table to drink.

Mr Smith opened proceedings by saying that they all got thirty per cent and Mr Smith got ten per cent. The boys agreed. They just had to figure out how to do it.

Sabini said, "what day is protection collection?"

"Friday afternoon," replied the other two.

That was in two day's time.

"What we will do is link up forces and collect on a Friday morning - this Friday."

Taff said, "we could all meet up in The Seven Stars. It's on the high street." The other two agreed. Mr Smith was listening, enthralled.

"They will come for us on Sunday," said Stuart.

"It's a declaration of war," said Taff.

"They can raise fifty to a hundred men," said Stuart.

"We will have to raise two hundred," said Sabini..."I can pay ten shillings a man," continued Sabini.

Then he asked Stuart and Taff if they could put some money in. The Scot and the Welshman would put up ten shillings a man as well. They were confident they could raise an army as well.

"We need guns," said Sabini.

"I will get those with Mr Smith, why do you think the Irish will come for us on Sunday?," continued Sabini.

"Well, they will be pissed off on Friday, Saturday will be the day to get their men and Sunday will be the day for the fight," said Taff.

The meeting was over. The three leaders had to buy their soldiers with money. Sabini went with Mr Smith to see Billy Bullet in Islington. He would buy four more guns and forty bullets for ten pounds. Mr Smith and Sabini then got back into the horse and carriage. Mr Smith was looking forward to the Santaniello family moving into his house on Wednesday. Sabini gave Mr Smith a five pound note to secure the services of the Metropolitan Police. They dropped off Mr Smith. He then told the coachman to go to Clerkenwell (as it was close by) where he could buy more jars of tomatoes and pasta. He also bought a big chunk of parmesan.

Sabini arrived back at headquarters at about six. The gang had gotten rid of a lot of raffle tickets. Tomorrow was the draw where the most popular gang member would 'win'. Bianchi was the last week's winner, so he wasn't allowed to participate in the election of the draw and you were not allowed to vote for yourself. Sabini then told everybody about the huge fight on Sunday. He also told everybody about the four extra guns he had bought.

The cooking was going on and everybody was having pork chops, bread and salad. Rossi mentioned the fact that with this morning's breakfast, there was a lot of pork being consumed. It was midweek and Massi mentioned the idea of maybe watching a football match. Sabini thought it was not a bad idea. Tomorrow would be recruitment day. Friday would be collection day in Holborn. Saturday would be collection day in Faringdon. Sunday would be the fight.

They all ate peacefully with no arguments. Then, as usual, the cards came out... Gerd the German would come into his own. He had been a bit quiet lately but was looking forward to the fight on Sunday. Sabini played cards as well. Bianchi played with a maximum loss of a pound. Everybody was flush with money. Sabini said that "there were no friends in cards" and the German agreed.

He and Sabini were getting close and there was mutual respect between the two. The German said he could get ten soldiers. Sabini needed at least fifty men. He would hope the Scot and the Welshman could get fifty men between them, making a total of about a hundred men (way short of his previous estimate). Sabini would be busy and maybe would have to delegate the recruitment to Bastoni and Gerd the German.

Bastoni asked "How many Irish do you think there will be?" Everybody thought between twenty-five and fifty. It was hard to say. They continued playing cards. Sabini won, so did the German. Only Caruso and Massi lost but not a great deal. Some made their way to bed. Some stayed chatting. They thought about Sunday. The last one when to bed at three am.

Thursday had arrived. It was raffle day and Sabini told the gang to sell the tickets. He met Mr Smith. The usual placid atmosphere. He brought along the German and Bastoni. They would share the carriage back to Islington and go on to Clerkenwell to do some recruiting for Sunday's mass brawl.

They arrived in Clerkenwell and went to all the shops trying to recruit soldiers. They didn't do too badly - they recruited twenty-two Italians and nine English men. He also told them to spread the word and to meet in The Seven Stars in Holborn at twilight on Sunday which would be about nine o'clock. Sabini thought if they didn't turn up he would go to Kilburn and collect protection money with his army (but it was only a thought).

Sabini, the German and Bastoni hailed a carriage to take them home. The German paid for the carriage. When they arrived it was time to vote who was the most popular in the raffle ticket income. There were three pounds five shillings and fourteen pennies to be had. It was won by the German who had eight votes. Caruso came second with four votes and he bought the wine.

Chapter Ten

Protection Money and Prostitution

It was Friday and Holborn was beckoning. Sabini had to meet up with Stuart and Taff. He brought the German and six others from his gang and they would meet with the Scots and the Welsh in The Seven Stars Public House. They walked three miles. They entered the pub and had some wine. There were eight of them. There were also nine Scots and seven Welshmen.

Sabini and everybody would have to know which shops paid the Irish protection money. There were about a hundred shops and business premises. The

Irish had about fifty per cent of the market or lost fifty per cent of the market. The boys just started on the shops closest to the pub and went along. They collected three shillings a shop.

It was one in the afternoon. The three gangs had to extort protection money before four o'clock, which is when the Irish gang turned up. The three gangs finished at half-past three. They had collected three hundred shillings. It turned out perfect as they had made fifteen pounds - a fiver a gang. The Scottish and the Welsh loved the German and wanted to buy him from Sabini but Sabini said no. The gangs split up and said they would meet on Sunday at twilight... I'm sure they would have loved to be a fly on the wall and see the Irish faces when they arrived!

They walked the forty-five minute journey back home to Soho but they were tired and were looking forward to their dinner. Caruso, Bastoni and Carlucci were looking forward to their night with the girls (only because they could reserve their chairs). Five of the gang were playing cards. Bianchi served up pasta and chicken. He didn't like making a sauce with chicken - he thought it made the sauce 'too orangey'.

Everybody ate and they had never been happier. Sabini could not believe how successful the gang had become. He touched some wood for luck. He thought about the Irish and how many soldiers they could muster. What sort of tactics they would use? Would they have guns?

Caruso, Bastoni and Carlucci were on pimping duty and had to mind the girls in their respective hotels. Carlucci had to get a horse and carriage from The Dorchester to the Savoy. Bastoni had to go to The Ritz where he thought about cocaine and Caruso went to The Dorchester. He also thought about cocaine.

It was about nine o'clock and Caruso had to mind six girls. Business was good and the girls were busy. Julia had already had two gentlemen. She then talked to Caruso about the idea of starting up a tailor and dressmaker. Caruso said it's all going to happen. Julia had a gin and Schweppes. Caruso had a glass of red wine. Caruso then asked Julia if she could find a madam.

The Dorchester was getting busy. One of the girls came down and complained that she got spanked and it hurt.

Caruso said, "Do you want me to sort him out?"

The girl said, "No, it's alright - I've had worse."

Caruso felt a bit strange because he fancied all of the girls. He had felt like this before and hated himself for feeling jealous; he loved Julia.

Bastoni went up to the bar in The Ritz and ordered his usual glass of red wine. The girls flocked to him except one who was upstairs. Bastoni wanted a bit of cocaine like he did last week. He spotted a gentleman with a little bit of white in his nostril.

Bastoni said, "could I have some white snuff?"

The gentleman said, "No, I haven't got enough."

Bastoni wanted to whack him.

"Can you get me some from somewhere else? I will give you ten shillings."

"Yes," the man said, "just wait here."

A few minutes later the man gave him quite a sizeable amount. Bastoni went from wanting to whack him to loving him. He went to the gentleman's toilet and snorted some. He then returned to the bar and talked to everyone. The girls he was minding were next to him. He offered the cocaine to the girls. They all took it except one. The night for Bastoni was a blinder and he started fancying his prostitutes. The bar was full of very rich men and it would be a good night for the Sabini organisation.

Carlucci was also after cocaine. He was lucky, one of the girls had some and Carlucci took some discreetly (even though it was legal). He then took some more at the bar. He had a permanent smile across his face.

Back at the house, the boys were playing cards. As usual, it was another showdown between Gerd, The Big German, and Sabini. The German had two pairs but Sabini had three fours. Sabini said in front of everybody that the German would be joint second-in-command with Caruso and Bastoni. The German said he wanted to do some pimping duties.

"We will see, whoever brings the least money from the hotels gets made redundant," said Sabini.

Caruso in The Dorchester started to become interested in what the girls did with the men. Julia came down.

Caruso asked, "what did you do with him?"

"I just chatted with him. He wanted to chat about his wife and kids. He seemed alright. He also gave me a five shilling tip."

Julia, if we get you this shop, will you stop this?"

"I don't know, I can do both jobs."

Back at The Ritz, Bastoni gave a couple of the girls some cocaine. Everybody seemed on form and the girls were letting business slip because they quite fancied Bastoni. Bastoni got more wine and chatted to a racehorse owner. He seemed a bit young to own a racehorse.

"How much did you pay for him?," said Bastoni.

The man said, "one thousand five hundred pounds."

"Is it any good?," said Bastoni.

"No, it's useless. It doesn't like leaving the stable. It has good breeding so I might retire it to stud."

"You have a lazy horse and it probably won't even do its own fucking," said Bastoni.

The racehorse owner bought himself and Bastoni. There was a stench of sterling in the air.

Carlucci was in The Savoy. He was talking to the girls and enquired if they thought they'd be busy. In The Savoy, sometimes, the men would give the girls 'white snuff' as a tip. Carlucci asked the girls if they had any. One of the girls said "yes" and gave it to him. Carlucci took it at the bar. He got talking to a stockbroker. He asked the stockbroker if there was a job for him (not that Carlucci ever wanted to be a stockbroker).

The stockbroker said, "I could probably get you a job on the Bombay Stock Exchange, it's only been open twenty-five years."

Carlucci went back to the girls with cocaine flooding his brain cells. The girls were busy. It was a good night.

Meanwhile back at the poker game in Soho. The Big German and Sabini were cleaning up. The German was now joint second-in-command with Caruso and Bastoni. Sabini asked The Big German if he wanted to become a pimp at Bailey's hotel. Bailey's Hotel was in South Kensington. Gerd The Big German was elated.

"When can I start?," said Gerd.

"Probably next week," said Sabini.

They carried on their absorbing poker game. Bianchi was dealing as a croupier. Again they suggested having a card school in Soho. They could charge five per cent of the pot.

There was no shortage of plans and plots with the organisation. Sabini's naivety kept him in good stead paradoxically as he never had any baggage or bitter feelings. The gang were really happy with him and he would abstain from the voting of the raffle draw ensuring somebody else would win.

The boys enjoyed their game of cards and the ones that weren't playing were learning chess, so one day they could eventually take on The Big German. Sabini thought about the Farringdon protection tomorrow, the meeting with the police officers and the big fight on Sunday. He would bring forward the moving in date for the Santaniellos for Mr Smith for Monday. Tuesday would be Sandown. Then a meeting with the Scots and the Welsh about expansion on Wednesday. Also on Wednesday, he would work on getting a tailors and a dressmakers as well as a brothel in Soho. He was busy.

Over at The Dorchester, the girls were busy too. Caruso had never seen anything like it. He was mostly by himself. He was at the bar drinking Chianti and thinking of the big fight with the Irish on Sunday in Holborn.

Julia came down smelling of The Dorchester's soap.

"Can you make me a suit?," asked Caruso to Julia.

"I can work with cotton or silk or wool," said Julia, "one for summer and one for winter. I really want to start work," said Julia.

Caruso was happy that Julia was reducing her hours as a prostitute.

"Would you consider me as a boyfriend if you didn't do what you do?," asked Caruso.

"Course I would, I think you're great and a good catch."

"I'm joint second-in-command now and really close to Sabini," said Caruso. He added, "In a couple of years I will have enough money to look after you."

Julia said, "In six months, I will have enough money to look after you."

Bastoni looked good in The Ritz. The girls were doing well and Bastoni was drinking a Sangiovese.

He always thought that when he was on his own, it meant that the girls were busy. Twenty minutes later, one of the girls turned up and said "The man paid me a pound and all he wanted to do was talk and put his arm around me. How gentle."

Bastoni thought it was quite interesting. He thought everything was interesting being coked out of his face as was Carlucci in The Savoy. The pimps found themselves getting closer to their girls.

All three had a good night where takings were concerned. Caruso took away fourteen pounds, Bastoni eleven and Carlucci twelve. Carlucci got a carriage back. Bastoni popped in The Dorchester to walk home with Caruso. They got home and everybody was in bed.

Chapter Eleven

Saturday and Sunday

Again Bianchi was the first up. The only thing on his mind was breakfast and dinner. He would buy four chickens and potatoes for a Saturday special. Massi didn't like chicken because of the way it looked.

The boys started coming down and the usual bacon and eggs greeted them. Bianchi was busy slicing a cottage loaf and drizzling a fair amount of olive oil on top. Caruso, Bastoni and Carlucci were still upstairs sleeping.

Bianchi said to Sabini, "Can we get coffee next week?"

"That's a good idea," said Sabini.

Sabini would look into it. The German asked if they could squeeze in a game of cards before then and Sabini agreed. The two boys were playing chess and were getting quite good.

It was time to leave Soho and go to Faringdon. It was a good two-mile walk going through Holborn. They had about seventy to eighty shops and business premises to go through, collecting the usual three shillings a shop. Sabini put everyone in groups of three but one shopkeeper and a confectioner did not want to pay. The Big German got him by the throat and said, "If you don't pay I will smash the shop up!"

The rest of the day went quite smoothly and they all went to the café to have coffee where they had just extorted three shillings. They didn't have their own coffee machine (they just made it manually with a strainer). The coffee stimulated them for their walk home. Some would have to go to Clerkenwell to get more recruits for Sunday's battle.

Sabini and all eight of them made their way to Clerkenwell. It was only a quarter of an hour on foot. The gang made their way to pubs, shops and cafés and some were on the street recruiting. It was slow going. Sabini was even asking non-Italians (and there were quite a few of them). The organisation went to a café for another coffee and a roll of cheese and ham.

They started walking up to men to see if they would except ten shillings for a short night's work. Sabini hoped that the Scottish leader and the Welsh leader would be recruiting themselves - it was important.

The Soho men worked hard all afternoon. Some of the men recruited their friends as a kind of knock-on effect. Men were coming out of their houses to be recruited. It was getting busier and at one stage there was even a queue. Sabini had to write all of the names down. The Big German also did well. The recruits were told they were fighting the Irish at Holborn and to meet at The Seven Stars Public House tomorrow night at twilight.

Again, Sabini and The Big German paced the streets looking for anyone. Before six o'clock they had forty-seven men on the list. Eighty per cent were Italian. The rest were English and Scottish. Sabini also had about twenty men recruited in the week. He wanted the biggest gang in London; it would be the biggest fight London had ever seen.

He needed a couple of carriages to take the boys back to Soho. They passed by and stopped. The boys got in and left Clerkenwell. It took a good forty minutes to get home. They had to go through Russell Square.

When they got home Caruso, Bastoni and Carlucci were up. All the gang were there. Bianchi was roasting chickens and potatoes. The atmosphere was tense except for Bastoni. He said to Sabini that he had a great strategy for defeating the Irish tomorrow night based on Hannibal's victory against the Romans in 216 B.C.

"They come in a square towards us and we've got a thin horizontal line. They attack our middle, we draw them in. Then our flanks (right and left) attack their sides and rear. The Irish in the middle are rendered useless."

That's a fucking great idea, Bastoni," said Sabini.

"How many men do you reckon they will have," said Gerd the German.

"I don't know," said Sabini.

"With our Hannibal tactic they will need four hundred men and even then we could do them," said Bastoni.

The atmosphere changed for the better after Bastoni's speech.

Bastoni said, "We will envelop them like a circle around a square."

The chicken and potatoes were succulent. The wine went down well. Bianchi asked Sabini if he could have an apprentice. Sabini said he might think about it.

Caruso, Bastoni and Carlucci were getting ready for their jobs at The Dorchester, The Ritz and The Savoy. The cards came out and Bianchi said that he spent most of the time by himself except when he went to Brighton Races.

The two lads were learning chess and were doing well and Gerd the German knew that soon they would muster up the confidence to take him on.

As usual, the cards came out because it was good fun. Bianchi insisted on playing and won a lot of money at the first hand with three kings. He won the second hand as well with two aces. Everybody was in a great mood apart from the ones that lost at cards.

The boys arrived at their respective hotels. Caruso and Julia spoke about getting her tailors and dressmakers shop amongst other things. The Dorchester was seeing a lot of people these days and the five girls were turning tricks to make it busier.

Caruso was on good form with Julia and really wanted her and hoped that Julia wanted him. Caruso ordered a glass of wine for himself, five gins and Schweppes for the girls. Julia then told Caruso if she got her shop and became a young madam, she would stop being one of the girls and buy a house with Caruso. She also told him that she could start up another tailors and dressmakers somewhere else like Mayfair and that she had money.

In The Ritz, Bastoni was there talking to his favourite Elizabeth. Bastoni loved her to bits. He asked her if she could get him some white snuff. Elizabeth said, "wait here. I will get you some."

She brought back loads and charged five shillings. Bastoni and Elizabeth both sniffed it together. Two of the other girls came over and had their gin and Schweppes and a sniff of the 'white snuff'. Bastoni then got talking to a gentleman who used to be a stockbroker and now worked for Lloyd's bank. He also had eight racehorses but on the whole, he was losing money. One horse though was outstanding and had won a classic race at Newmarket - the 2000 Guineas.

Bastoni seemed quite happy. He told the girls that tomorrow night he might not come, but if he did it might be at about 12 pm.

In The Savoy, Carlucci went straight up to Alice and said hello and told her he might not make it Sunday night but he never told her why. Alice said if he didn't come she would keep onto the money until she next saw him. He bought the girls some drinks and they talked about what they would do when they finished. Sleep was the best option. Sometimes they would go to Alice's flat near Hyde Park. One of the girls gave Carlucci a sniff of cocaine. Carlucci thought that they were all winners in The Savoy.

Sabini was playing cards. The Big German was not playing but holding court. He was also watching the chess match. He was quite impressed with the two lads learning and playing Chess.

Out of the blue, Sabini said, "We will play for another half hour and then go to The Ritz."

Everybody cheered apart from the ones that were losing at cards. The chess players said that if there wasn't a winner in the allocated time they would leave the chess pieces where they were, and resume later.

Sabini then left with the gang to go to The Dorchester. There were thirteen of them walking.

Sabini thought they might as well have a long night as they all had to be on form late for Sunday night's big fight.

Caruso loved seeing the gang in The Dorchester. He truly did. He spoke to Caruso who pointed out the five girls. Julia came over. They had met before. Julia enquired about the possibility of tailors and dressmakers in Soho. Sabini said that it was a brilliant idea. Sabini got the drinks for everybody; they had truly arrived.

Sabini told everybody to see if the gentleman at The Dorchester were interested in an imminent card school in Soho. If he said yes, then they would telegram them with the time and place. They needed names and addresses. In about an hour they got four names and addresses. The German got three of the names and addresses. Rossi and Bianchi were too busy chatting up some girls. The place looked packed. It was only two in the morning. He asked everybody except Caruso if they wanted to go to The Ritz. Rossi, Bianchi and some others wanted to stay in The Dorchester. Sabini then left with The Big German and others to walk to The Ritz.

They all sauntered in and Sabini saw Bastoni at the bar. Sabini loved Bastoni because he could think outside the box. Everybody went to Bastoni. Bastoni wiped what he thought was possibly cocaine from his nose. He was with Elizabeth talking about a high-class brothel in Soho. Sabini ordered two bottles of Sangiovese, five gin and Schweppes. Alice liked the idea of a brothel. She also liked the idea of working at The Ritz.

Sabini got Gerd The Big German. He also told Bastoni to drum up business for the card school. Sabini told him to get names and addresses for the telegram. Gerd did not disappoint. He got four more potential card players. Bastoni went into the gents to do some 'white snuff'. He just thought it would be in keeping with the unwritten rules of the gang if he didn't tell anybody. He never knew that Carlucci was on it, nor did Carlucci know that Bastoni was on it - it was just sheer coincidence. The gang managed to find a table. Sabini and the

German sat next to each other talking about expansion.

Bastoni was at the bar again and found two card players without even trying. Three of the girls came over and they asked who Sabini was.

Sabini got up and said, "it's me."

"You look like a leader," said one of the girls.

"Thank you," said Sabini. "Your drinks are at the bar," he added.

Sabini thought it best if he and Gerd went to The Savoy and see Carlucci. Sabini would call The Big

German, Gerd. They got into a horse and carriage. The Savoy was half an hour away. It was near The Strand and close to the river.

They walked and Carlucci was talking to Alice. Sabini and Gerd fell in love with her.

"How can you not fall in love with her?," asked Gerd to Carlucci.

"Who says I'm not in love?," asked Caruso.

"Don't tell me you want a gin and Schweppes?," said Sabini.

"Where are the others?," added Sabini.

"They will be down soon."

Sabini left to get wine and gin and Schweppes. Carlucci went to the gents to do his 'white snuff'.

It was nearly home time and it was a big day for everyone tomorrow. Sabini collected thirteen pounds and said to the girls that they might be late tomorrow. Sabini, Gerd and Carlucci got a carriage to The Ritz. They collected fourteen pounds. They then told the girls there as well that they might be late tomorrow. Then they walked to The Dorchester. They told the girls the same about Sunday's possible absence and collected fifteen pounds. Everybody got home at about six in the morning.

Sunday arrived and everybody had a late breakfast. The last of the boys came down at about twelve. He made the bacon crispy as everybody liked it. Bianchi was in a great mood because he got the name and the address of a girl he met last night. He would send her a telegram, later on, that day from the telegraph office not very far away. Bianchi waited and said to Rossi if he would do the washing up for sixpence. Rossi agreed. Bianchi ran to the telegraph office.

Everybody knew it was a big night. It could either make them or break them. The cards were dealt and Bianchi had returned. Gerd, The Big German, was winning. Sabini was winning but not as much. Carlucci was level. The others were losing a bit. Time passed and it was now seven o'clock and Sabini said we will go soon, but not before a tutorial on the reloading of the guns. Sabini had eight guns. He kept one for himself and gave one to Gerd, Caruso, Bastoni, Carlucci, Rossi, Massi and Marchisio. Then they walked to Holborn.

When they got to The Seven Stars they were amazed to see so many men. They had nearly all turned up. The Scottish leader had posted four scouts on a relay system to see if the Irish were coming. The scouts had bells so they could warn Sabini's army through sound that the Irish were coming even if they were a mile away. More men from Clerkenwell turned up. Stuart, the Scot, and Taff had paid their soldiers. Sabini paid him as well - it cost him nearly thirty pounds. The atmosphere was tense.

Bastoni explained with a pen and bit of paper the tactics they would use. He drew a square for the Irish and a long line for the alliance. Stuart and Taff had handpicked the men that would be in the middle. Sabini wanted to be in the middle. They would be the most vulnerable.

The bells rang. The Irish were less than a mile away. The Alliance formed their horizontal line. It was a deathly quiet and they could hear the sound of hobnail boots.

The Irish came within sight and reformed into a neatly packed square. There were about a hundred and fifty Irishmen. There were about a hundred and thirty men in Sabini's army.

The Irish kept on walking to within fifty yards and when they came within the thirty yards, the Irish square stopped. There was no longer the sound of hobnail boots, or voices or the sounds of a horse and carriage. None of the two hundred and eighty men made a noise. It was a quiet of surreal proportions. Then an Irishman stepped out…

Printed in Great Britain
by Amazon